Dear St. Jude Nursery School Children,

Catch your dreams!

Rainbow Star Wishes,
Michelle Zimmerman

Can't
Catch a
Butterfly

Can't Catch a Butterfly

By Michelle Zimmerman

Rainbow Star Books

Rainbow Star Inc. — New York
Children's Educational Resources

Can't Catch A Butterfly
Published by Rainbow Star Inc.

Copyright © 2008 by Rainbow Star Inc.
First Printing, April 2008

Publisher's Cataloging-in-Publication Data
(Provided by Quality Books, Inc.)

Zimmerman, Michelle.
    Can't catch a butterfly / by Michelle Zimmerman.
    p. cm.
    SUMMARY: A little boy chases colorful butterflies
"over a hill," "under a bush," high and low, in this
rhyming story.
    Audience: Ages 2-7.
    LCCN 2007942623
    ISBN-13: 978-0-9802363-0-9
    ISBN-10: 0-9802363-0-4

    1. Butterflies--Juvenile fiction. 2. Colors--
Juvenile fiction. 3. Space perception--Juvenile
fiction. [1. Butterflies--Fiction. 2. Color--Fiction.
3. Space perception--Fiction. 4. Stories in rhyme.]
I. Title.

PZ8.3.Z498Can 2008   [E]
                              QBI07-600346

Creative Team
Michelle Zimmerman: Text/Illustrations
Diane Burgwin: Literacy Specialist
Janet Enser: Literacy Specialist/Editor
Tom Fallica: Consulting Editor
Birgitta Millard: Creative Director

PRINTED IN THE UNITED STATES OF AMERICA

Rainbow Star Inc.
P.O. Box 422 Centereach, NY 11720

Rainbow Star Books logo is a trademark of Rainbow Star Inc.

Visit us at www.rainbowstarbooks.com

To my husband for helping me "catch" my dreams.

To Christopher & Amanda:
Keep SOARING like a butterfly!

– M.Z.

I'm ready. All set!
Let's catch butterflies with my net!

Blue butterfly, where can you be?

I'm flying high in the sky.
You can't catch me.

Pink butterfly,
where can you be?

I'm fluttering low in the grass.
You can't catch me.

Green butterfly,
    where can you be?

I'm dancing on the water.
You can't catch me.

Purple butterfly,
where can you be?

I'm twirling next to a flower.
You can't catch me.

Orange butterfly,
where can you be?

I'm hiding in the tree.
You can't catch me.

Yellow butterfly,
where can you be?

I'm resting under a bush.
You can't catch me.

Red butterfly,
where can you be?

I'm floating over a hill.
You can't catch me.

I caught all the butterflies.
One, two, three.

They're locked in a box
for me to see.

Please, little boy.
Let us out with the key.

I don't want you to go.
Won't you stay?

Oh, gee.

Thank you, little boy.
We are free!
WE ARE FREE!

Can you find the...

orange butterfly

red butterfly

blue butterfly

black butterfly

pink butterfly

green butterfly

yellow butterfly

purple butterfly

brown butterfly

Children are our brightest stars. Each little being is a brilliant creation. They shine of promise, potential, and possibilities as endless as a rainbow. **Rainbow Star Books** believes that reading truly is the foundation of education. We feature engaging stories to highlight the joy of books while improving reading readiness skills. Our company's mission is to help children shine their brightest through language, literacy, laughter, and love. To reach this goal, we are dedicated to empowering families, educators, and extended caregivers with a full spectrum of multimedia learning tools with each publication. **Rainbow Star Books** is committed to coloring a youngster's world with high quality educational resources to promote bold, confident communicators.

Free coloring sheets and teaching tools for *Can't Catch a Butterfly* are available at our online store:

www.RainbowStarBooks.com

Get ready for more adventures
    with the little boy...coming soon!